W9-BFW-762

The Curious Little Dolphin

Ariane Chottin
Adapted by Patricia Jensen
Illustrations by Olivier Raquois

Reader's Digest Kids
Pleasantville, N.Y. – Montreal

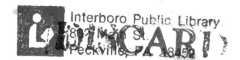

One day at the end of summer, a curious little dolphin named Scooter was swimming with his mother and grandmother.

"I can't wait to begin our trip!" Scooter said excitedly. "When will we leave, Mama?"

"Tonight," his mother answered. "But it will take a long time to reach the warm water down south."

"I don't care how long it takes!" cried Scooter, flipping through the air. "Besides, I'm going to swim faster than anyone else!"

"Now, Scooter," said his grandmother. "We all must travel together. That is the best way to protect ourselves from danger."

"That's right, Scooter," his mother agreed. "And you must be especially careful to stay with the group because you are so small."

But Scooter was too excited to listen. All he could think about was surfing on the waves and riding the warm currents.

That evening, the dolphins left for the warm waters of the South.

"Watch this!" Scooter called to his best friend, Splash. Splash laughed as Scooter jumped high in the air, landing far away from the others.

"Scooter!" his mother called instantly.
"Don't swim over there! If a shark spots
you off by yourself, you will be in terrible
danger."

"Just wait till we get down south,"
Scooter whispered to Splash. "Then we can
go off and explore everything all by
ourselves."

The band of dolphins swam and swam. After many days and nights, the water began to get warmer. Soon Scooter and Splash saw a small group of islands in the distance.

"We're here!" shouted Scooter happily. "Mama, can I go play with Splash?"

"Not now, Scooter," answered his mother. "We're all tired from our long trip. There will be plenty of time to play tomorrow."

When the sun rose the next morning, Scooter's mother had to go hunt for food.

"Stay here with your grandmother," she told Scooter. "I'll take you exploring when I get back."

Scooter tried to wait for his mother to return, but he was just too curious. As soon as his grandmother wasn't looking, Scooter swam off to find Splash.

Scooter and Splash swam and played for
hours. Then Scooter noticed an underwater
cave.

"Splash!" he called. "Come look at what
I've found!"

The two little dolphins stuck their noses
inside the entrance to the cave. Sunlight
played off the sides of the cave, splashing
beautiful colors everywhere.

"Isn't it wonderful?" exclaimed Scooter.
"Let's go inside."

Scooter and Splash swam into the cave.
There they saw yellow and black clown fish
swimming by and red sea anemones waving
their tiny tentacles. As they swam deeper
into the cave, the water became darker
and darker.

"What's that over there?" Splash asked
nervously. "I see two shining eyes."

Scooter looked up just in time to see a huge shark swimming rapidly toward them.

"Oh, no!" he cried. "A shark!"

Scooter and Splash flipped their tails and swam at full speed toward the cave entrance.

"Help!" the two little dolphins called desperately as they sped out of the cave. "Help us!"

All the adult dolphins suddenly surrounded Scooter and Splash, frightening the shark away. Scooter swam slowly over to his mother and said, "I'm sorry."

As angry as his mother was, she softened. "It's hard not to be curious when there are so many things to see and do," she said gently. "But from now on..."

"We'll do them together!" Scooter said with a smile.

Although they live in water, dolphins are not fish. They are mammals, which means that they breathe air and nurse their young. Baby dolphins stay with their mothers for more than a year.

Dolphins breathe through an opening, called a blow-hole, at the top of their heads. The blow-hole opens to let air in and out and closes when the dolphin's head is under water.

A dolphin's ears are very small—just two tiny holes, one behind each eye. Nevertheless, dolphins hear ten times better than people do!